Up in a Rocket

Written by Jill Atkins

Illustrated by Davide Ortu

Collins

I had a rocket.

My rocket was ...

4

5

My rocket shot up and off.

I met Zang.

We had fun.

We had melon fizz.

My rocket shot off and up.

My rocket was not big.

/z/

/zz/

14

/ng/

 After reading

Letters and Sounds: Phase 3

Word count: 40

Focus phonemes: /w/ /z/ zz /sh/ /ng/

Common exception words: was, my, we, I

Curriculum links: Mathematics: children use everyday language to talk about size ... to compare quantities and objects

Early learning goals: Listening and attention: listen to stories, accurately anticipating key events and respond to what is heard with relevant comments, questions or actions; Understanding: answer 'how' and 'why' questions about experiences and in response to stories or events; Reading: children use phonic knowledge to decode regular words and read them aloud accurately; they demonstrate understanding when talking with others about what they have read

Developing fluency

- Your child may enjoy hearing you read the story.
- Model reading the story using expression. Ask your child to read some of the story again, using lots of expression.

Phonic practice

- Look at the word **ping** together. Sound talk it together, 'p-i-ng', and point out to your child the /ng/ sound. Now blend the sounds together 'ping'.
- Ask your child to do the same with the word **Zang**. Can they think of other words that contain the 'ng' sound? (*thing, ring, string*)
- Now look at 'I spy sounds' on pages 14–15. How many words can your child spot that have the /z/ or /zz/ sound in them? How about words that contain the /ng/ sound? (*fizz, buzz, zip, drawing, king*)

Extending vocabulary

- Read each of the following words to your child. Can they tell you a word that is the opposite of each one?

1. big (*small*)   2. up (*down*)   3. sad (*happy*)